Alf Prøysen
Stories for Christmas

Alf Prøysen

Stories for Christmas

Illustrated by
Kari Grossman

Translated by
Patricia Crampton and Marianne Helweg

Hutchinson
London Melbourne Auckland Johannesburg

First published in Great Britain in 1987 by Hutchinson Children's Books
An imprint of Century Hutchinson Ltd
Brookmount House, 62–65 Chandos Place,
Covent Garden, London WC2N 4NW

Century Hutchinson Australia (Pty) Ltd
16–22 Church Street, Hawthorn, Melbourne, Victoria 3122

Century Hutchinson New Zealand Limited
32–34 View Road, PO Box 40–086, Glenfield, Auckland 10

Century Hutchinson South Africa (Pty) Ltd
PO Box 337, Bergvlei 2012, South Africa

Printed and bound in Great Britain by W. S. Cowell, Ipswich

British Library Cataloguing in Publication Data
Prøysen, Alf
    Stories for Christmas
    I. Title   II. Grossman, Kari   III. Alf
    Prøysen Jule-bok. *English*
    839.8′2374[J]   PZ7

ISBN 0-09-172100-8

Contents

The little town that forgot it was Christmas

High up on the hillside stood a little town, all by itself.

The people who lived there were exactly like other people in other towns. Some were tall and some were small; some were hard-working and some were lazy; some liked fish cakes better than meatballs and some liked meatballs better than fish cakes. So there were a few differences between them, but in one respect they were all alike.

They were terribly forgetful, and they forgot the most extraordinary things, all at the same time!

Once they forgot to put on their shoes. It had

been very warm all that summer and they had gone about barefoot. But when autumn came they forgot to put their shoes on.

'Heavens above, how cold it is!' they said to each other. 'Well, I really don't know what will happen if it gets colder than it is now. And it will be worse when the snow comes.'

And when the snow came they walked out in their bare feet, exclaiming: 'Aah, it must be well below freezing now!' And off they walked, their feet as cold as ice.

One day, when two old women were chatting at the crossroads, with ice-cold feet, they caught sight of a boy talking to the blacksmith. 'Why are you putting shoes on that horse?' said the boy. And at once the old women remembered that they had forgotten to put on their own shoes.

The old women ran home and put their shoes on and after that one of them walked eastward and the other walked westward, telling all the townsfolk why their feet were so cold. And all the townsfolk put their shoes on at once.

Another time, they had all forgotten to eat. They went without food for several days, till at last they all fell ill and had to go to bed and ring for the doctor. But the doctor could not come, because he too had forgotten to eat, so he was as ill as all the others.

But one day the doctor caught a glimpse of a little mouse running off with a bit of cheese in its mouth, and then he remembered what it was they had forgotten to do.

So up he got and had a meal, and after that he travelled round visiting the sick throughout the town and told them that they had simply forgotten to eat. At that they all got out of bed and had a good meal and soon felt well again.

But the worst time of all was when they forgot that it would soon be Christmas.

On Christmas Eve no one had swept their house and hung up new curtains and no one had brought in their Christmas tree and there was not so much as a single Father Christmas mask in the shop windows. The school children started the day by singing, 'Summer suns are glowing,' and there was not so much as a single crumb of cake in a single cake tin in all the town.

In a little room at the very top of the town, right at the edge of the forest, a little girl sat thinking. She was only five years old and she usually jumped and danced and played and had fun, but now she just thought and thought. At last she went to the wood and stood looking at all the little prickly fir trees.

'There's something we've forgotten again,' said the little girl to herself, 'and it's something to do with a little fir tree, but I can't remember what is is.'

So the little girl went back to her house and found a pair of scissors and some tissue paper. 'It's something to do with scissors, too,' she said. 'But I can't remember what it is.'

Then the little girl went to the barn, and there she saw a sheaf of corn which her father had hung up high under a beam so that the mice would not get it.

'It's something to do with that corn as well,' said the girl, and as she stood there looking about her she saw the long pole on which they always hung the sheaf of corn for the birds to eat at Christmas time. Then the little girl remembered that it was almost Christmas Day!

'Oh, it's Christmas Eve, it's Christmas Eve!' she cried, and ran in to tell her mother and father, but they were not at home. 'Oh, how am I going to tell the whole town that it will soon be Christmas? How am I to tell everyone in town that it's Christmas Eve?' cried the little girl.

She tried to lift the long pole and hang the Christmas sheaf on top of it, but it was too much

for her. Then she had an idea: the flagpole! She could hoist the Christmas sheaf on the flagpole!

That was not too difficult, and as soon as she had done it a little bluetit flew down from the topmost twig of the tallest fir tree, sending the snow tumbling down its trunk.

'Where are you going, where are you going?' twittered the other bluetits, who had been dozing among the branches.

'It's Christmas, it's Christmas, the little girl has put up the Christmas sheaf!' he called.

'We're coming too, we're coming too,' sang

the other bluetits, and off they flew.

The telephonists ran to the windows of the telephone exchange to see where the birds were going and then they too saw the Christmas sheaf on the flagpole. In a moment they were ringing up everyone in town, to tell them they had forgotten that Christmas was coming.

And the people started roasting and boiling and frying; some of them swept the houses and some hung up fresh curtains and some went out to the woods to cut Christmas trees and some wrapped up the Christmas presents they had hidden away before they began to forget, and some hung up Christmas stars in the windows.

At last all the townsfolk climbed up into a gigantic bathtub which the carpenter had been making while the others cleaned and swept and baked for Christmas, and they all had a bath together.

At the very moment when they had finished and put on their clean clothes, and the mother of the little girl in the cottage at the top of the town was tying a red ribbon in her hair . . . at that very moment, the church bells rang out and it was Christmas Day.

Anderson the carpenter and Father Christmas

There was once a carpenter called Anderson. He was a good father and he had a lot of children.

One Christmas Eve, while his wife and children were decorating the Christmas tree, Anderson crept out to his woodshed. He had a surprise for them all: he was going to dress up as Father Christmas, load a sack of presents on to his sledge and go and knock on the front door. But as he pulled the loaded sledge out of the woodshed, he slipped and fell right across the sack of presents. This set the sledge moving, because the ground sloped from the shed down to the road, and Anderson had no time even to shout, 'Way there!' before he crashed into another sledge, coming down the road.

'I'm very sorry,' said Anderson.

'Don't mention it; I couldn't stop myself,' said the other man. Like Anderson, he was dressed in Father Christmas clothes and had a sack on his sledge.

'We seem to have had the same idea,' said
Anderson. 'I see you're all dressed up like me.'
He laughed and shook the other man's hand.
'My name's Anderson.'

'Glad to meet you,' said the other. 'I'm Father
Christmas.'

'Ha, ha!' laughed Anderson. 'You will have
your little joke, and quite right too on a Christmas Eve.'

'That's what I thought,' said the other man,
'and if you agree we can change places tonight,
and that will be a better joke still; I'll take the
presents along to *your* children, if you'll go and
visit *mine*. But you must take off that costume.'

Anderson looked a bit puzzled. 'What am I to
dress up in then?'

'You don't need to dress up at all,' said the
other. 'My children see Father Christmas all the
year round, but they've never seen a real
carpenter. I told them last Christmas that if they
were good this year I'd try and get the carpenter

to come and see them while I went round with presents for the other children.'

So he really *is* Father Christmas, thought Anderson to himself. Out loud he said: 'All right, if you really want me to, I will. The only thing is, I haven't any presents for your children.'

'Presents?' said Father Christmas. 'Aren't you a carpenter?'

'Yes, of course.'

'Well, then, all you have to do is to take along a few pieces of wood and some nails. You have a knife, I suppose?' Anderson said he had and went to look for the things in his workshop.

'Just follow my footsteps in the snow; they'll lead you to my house in the forest,' said Father Christmas. 'Then I'll take your sack and sledge and go and knock on your door.'

'Righto!' said the carpenter.

Then Father Christmas went off to knock at Anderson's door, and the carpenter trudged through the snow following Father Christmas's footsteps. They led him into the forest, past two pine trees, a large boulder and a tree stump. There, peeping out from behind the stump, were three little faces with red caps on.

'He's here! He's here!' shouted the Christmas

children as they scampered in front of him to a fallen tree, lying with its roots in the air. When Anderson followed them round to the other side of the roots he found Mother Christmas standing there waiting for him.

'Here he is, Mum! Here's the carpenter Dad promised us! Look at him! Isn't he tall!' The children were all shouting at once.

'Now, now, children,' said Mother Christmas, 'anybody would think you'd never seen a human being before.'

'We've never seen a proper *carpenter* before!' shouted the children. 'Come on in, Mr Carpenter!'

Pulling a branch aside, Mother Christmas led the way into the house. Anderson had to bend his long back double and crawl on his hands and knees. But once in, he found he could straighten up. The room had a mud floor, but it was very cosy, with tree stumps for chairs, and beds made of moss with covers of plaited grass. In the smallest bed lay the Christmas baby and in the far corner sat a very old Grandfather Christmas, his red cap nodding up and down.

'Has anyone come to see me?' croaked old Grandfather Christmas.

Mother Christmas shouted in his ear. 'It's

Anderson, the carpenter!' She explained that Grandfather was so old he never went out any more. 'He'd be pleased if you came over and shook hands with him.'

So Anderson took the old man's hand which was as hard as a piece of bark.

'Come and sit here, Mr Carpenter!' called the children.

The eldest one spoke first. 'D'you know what I want you to make for me? A toboggan. Can you do that – a little one, I mean?'

'I'll try,' said Anderson, and it didn't take long before he had a smart toboggan just ready to fly over the snow.

'Now it's my turn,' said the little girl who had pigtails sticking straight out from her head. 'I want a doll's bed.'

'Have you any dolls?' asked Anderson.

'No, but I borrow the fieldmice sometimes, and I can play with the baby squirrels as much as I like. They *love* being dolls. Please make me a doll's bed.'

So the carpenter made her a doll's bed. Then he asked the smaller boy what he would like. But he was very shy and could only whisper, 'Don't know.'

''Course he knows!' said his sister. 'He said it

just before you came. Go on, tell the carpenter.'

'A top,' whispered the little boy.

'That's easy,' said the carpenter, and in no time at all he had made a top.

'And now you must make something for Mum!' said the children. Mother Christmas had been watching, but all the time she held something behind her back.

'Shush, children, don't keep bothering the carpenter,' she said.

'That's all right,' said Anderson. 'What would you like me to make?'

Mother Christmas brought out the thing she was holding; it was a wooden ladle, very worn, with a crack in it.

'Could you mend this for me, d'you think?' she asked.

'Hm, hm!' said Anderson, scratching his ear with his carpenter's pencil. 'I think I'd better make you a new one.' And he quickly cut a new ladle for Mother Christmas. Then he found a long twisted root with a crook at one end and started stripping it with his knife. But, although the children asked him and asked him, he wouldn't tell them what it was going to be. When it was finished he held it up; it was a very distinguished-looking walking stick.

'Here you are, Grandpa!' he shouted to the old man, and handed him the stick. Then he gathered up all the chips and made a wonderful little bird with wings outspread to hang over the baby's cot.

'How pretty!' exclaimed Mother Christmas and all the children. 'Thank the carpenter nicely now. We'll certainly never forget this Christmas Eve, will we?'

'Thank you, Mr Carpenter. Thank you very much!' shouted the children.

There was a sound of feet stamping the snow off outside the door, and Anderson knew it was time for him to go. He said goodbye all round and wished them a Happy Christmas. Then he crawled through the narrow opening under the fallen tree. Father Christmas was waiting for him. He had the sledge and the empty sack with him.

'Thank you for your help, Anderson,' he said. 'What did the youngsters say when they saw you?'

'Oh, they seemed very pleased. Now they're just waiting for you to come home and see their new toys. How did you get on at my house? Was little Peter frightened of you?'

'Not a bit,' said Father Christmas. 'He

thought I was you. "Sit on Dadda's knee," he kept saying.'

'Well, I must get back to them,' said Anderson, and said goodbye to Father Christmas.

When he got home, the first thing he said to the children was, 'Can I see the presents you got from Father Christmas?'

But the children laughed. 'Silly! You've seen them already – when you were Father Christmas; you unpacked them all for us!'

'What would you say if I told you I had been with Father Christmas's family all this time?'

But the children laughed again. 'Where do they live, then?' they said.

'Just along there and over there,' said Anderson, pointing.

But it was snowing harder and harder, and very soon all of his own tracks and Father Christmas's had gone.

Mrs Pepperpot and the Christmas shopping

Once upon a time there was an old woman who went to bed one evening, as old women do, and woke up the next morning, as old women do – but then she found that she had become as small as a pepperpot, and no old women ever do that.

'What a nuisance! Today of all days,' said the old woman, and she climbed up the bedpost and swung her legs.

She wanted to buy a sheaf of corn for the birds' Christmas dinner, and she wanted to get them a little birdhouse where she could feed them every day. The other thing she wanted was a wreath of mistletoe to hang over the door, so that she could wish Mr Pepperpot a 'Happy Christmas' with a kiss. But Mr Pepperpot thought this was a silly idea.

'Quite unnecessary!' he said.

But Mrs Pepperpot was very clever at getting her own way; so even though she was now no bigger than a mouse, she soon worked out a plan. She heard her husband put his knapsack

22

down on the floor in the kitchen and she slid down the bedpost, scuttled over the doorstep and climbed into one of the knapsack pockets.

Mr Pepperpot put the knapsack on his back and set off through the snow on his sledge, while all the time Mrs Pepperpot peeped out from the pocket.

'Look at all those nice cottages!' she said to herself.

'I'll bet every one of them has a sheaf of corn and a little house for the birds. And they'll have mistletoe over the door as well, no doubt. But you wait till I get home; I'll show them!'

At the market there were crowds of people, both big and small; everyone shopping, and there was plenty to choose from! At one stall stood a farmer selling beautiful golden sheaves of corn. As her husband walked past the stall Mrs Pepperpot climbed out from the knapsack pocket and disappeared inside the biggest sheaf of all.

'Hullo, Mr Pepperpot,' said the farmer, 'how about some corn for the birds this Christmas?'

'Too dear!' answered Mr Pepperpot gruffly.

'Oh no, it's not!' squeaked the little voice of Mrs Pepperpot.

'If you don't buy this sheaf of corn I'll tell

everyone you're married to the woman who shrinks!'

Now Mr Pepperpot above all hates people to know about his wife turning small, so when he saw her waving to him from the biggest sheaf he said to the farmer: 'I've changed my mind; I'll have that one, please!'

But the farmer told him he would have to wait in the queue.

Only one little girl saw Mrs Pepperpot slip out of the corn and dash into a birdhouse on Mr Anderson's stall. He was a carpenter and made all his birdhouses look just like real little houses

with doors and windows for the birds to fly in and out. Of course Mrs Pepperpot chose the prettiest house; it even had curtains in the windows and from behind these she watched her husband buy the very best sheaf of corn and stuff it in his knapsack.

He thought his wife was safe inside and was just about to get on his sledge and head for home, when he heard a little voice calling from the next stall.

'Hullo, Husband!' squeaked Mrs Pepperpot, 'Haven't you forgotten something? You were going to buy me a birdhouse!'

Mr Pepperpot hurried over to the stall. He pointed to the house with the curtains and said: 'I want to buy that one, please!'

Mr Anderson was busy with his customers. 'You'll have to take your turn,' he said.

So once more poor Mr Pepperpot had to stand patiently in a queue. He hoped that no one else would buy the house with his wife inside.

But she wasn't inside; she had run out of the back door, and now she was on her way to the next stall. Here there was a pretty young lady selling holly and mistletoe. Mrs Pepperpot had to climb up the post to reach the nicest wreath, and there she stayed hidden.

Soon Mr Pepperpot came by, carrying both the sheaf of corn and the little birdhouse.

The young lady gave him a dazzling smile and said: 'Oh, Mr Pepperpot, wouldn't you like to buy a wreath of mistletoe for your wife?'

'No thanks,' said Mr Pepperpot, 'I'm in a hurry.'

'Swing high! Swing low! I'm in the mistletoe!' sang Mrs Pepperpot from her lofty perch.

When Mr Pepperpot caught sight of her his mouth fell open: 'Oh dear!' he groaned, 'This is too bad!'

With a shaking hand he paid the young lady

the right money and lifted the wreath down himself, taking care that Mrs Pepperpot didn't slip out of his fingers. This time there would be no escape; he would take his wife straight home, whether she liked it or not. But just as she was leaving, the young lady said: 'Oh, sir, you're our one hundredth customer, so you get a free balloon!' and she handed him a red balloon.

Before anyone could say 'Jack Robinson' Mrs Pepperpot had grabbed the string and, while Mr Pepperpot was struggling with his purse, gloves and parcels, his tiny wife was soaring up into the sky. Up she went over the marketplace, and soon she was fluttering over the trees of the forest, followed by a crowd of crows and magpies and small birds of every sort.

'Here I come!' she shouted in bird language. For, when Mrs Pepperpot was small, she could talk with animals and birds.

A big crow cawed: 'Are you going to the moon with that balloon?' 'Not quite, I hope!' said Mrs Pepperpot, and she told them the whole story. The birds all squawked with glee when they heard about the corn and the birdhouse she had got for them.

'But first you must help me,' said Mrs Pepperpot. 'I want you all to hang on to this balloon string and guide me back to land on my own doorstep.'

So the birds clung to the string with their beaks and claws and, as they flew down to Mrs Pepperpot's house, the balloon looked like a kite with fancy bows tied to its tail.

When Mrs Pepperpot set foot on the ground she instantly grew to her normal size. So she waved goodbye to the birds and went indoors to wait for Mr Pepperpot.

It was late in the evening before Mr Pepperpot came home, tired and miserable after searching everywhere for his lost wife. He put his knapsack down in the hall and carried the sheaf of corn and the birdhouse outside. But when he came in again he noticed that the mistletoe had disappeared. 'Oh well,' he said sadly, 'what does it matter now that Mrs Pepperpot is gone?'

He opened the door into the kitchen; there was the mistletoe hanging over the doorway and, under it, as large as life, stood Mrs Pepperpot!

'Darling Husband!' she said, as she put her arms round his neck and gave him a great big smacking kiss:

'Happy Christmas!'

Christmas decorations and sausages

The prettiest Christmas tree I've ever seen in my life was the one in Svingen, and the Christmas tree grew prettier and prettier every year. It reached right up to the roof and was laden with tinsel and glass balls, paper baskets and candles.

A week before Christmas the whole family would decorate the Christmas tree: husband and wife, the grown-up son and the three children. And all the rest of us children who lived in the neighbourhood of Svingen were allowed to come and watch.

'Just put the cover over the bed now, and they can look on,' said the wife. We clambered up and piled on to the bed, pushing and shoving to make room for all of us. We did not say a word, we just looked. Looked and looked, until someone knocked on the window and called our names. Messengers from home, big brothers and sisters who were supposed to bring us back to everyday life, to wood chopping and the evening meal and our homework.

29

'Why can't we have a Christmas tree like the one they've got in Svingen?' we children would say, as we sat in our thick jerseys eating sausages.

'Well – if you'd rather be freezing cold and have nothing to eat. . . .'

And that was explanation enough for us. We accepted it because we realized we were better off than the people in Svingen. We were better off than many other people too, and our mother always gave some meat and a little milk to those who had none. That is what it means to be well off, we children thought, as we walked through the dusk taking goodies to those who were hard up. The old woman who lived in the forest folded her hands and wept when we came. We felt quite like angels, standing at the door and hearing how good we were.

Then there was only Svingen left. Mother had sent us off with sausages to deliver there too.

'We've brought a bit of Christmas food for you,' we said, when we reached them.

'Thank you very much, put the sausages on the table,' said the old woman. Her husband set out chairs for us and we sat back and waited for the same thanks that we had received from the others to whom we had brought Christmas goodies.

31

But the little daughter only flew across the room and flung open the door into the cold living room.

There stood the Christmas tree, with the prettiest, most sparkling decorations you could possibly imagine.

It was we who were the poor ones, for the glory of Christmas was up there in Svingen, we thought.

And we walked quietly home and ate our sausages.

The little boy and the Christmas train

Once upon a time there was a young girl who was going into town on the Sunday before Christmas to look at the shops. As she crossed the road she saw a little boy in grey clothes, sitting on the side of a snowplough, swinging his legs.

The girl stopped, because she had never seen the little boy before and she knew that when you were as small as he was you should not be out alone after dark. 'Why are you sitting here?' she asked.

'No reason really,' said the boy, in a very thin, strange voice.

'Have your father and mother left you to look at the Christmas display?' asked the girl. 'Come along with me now, we'll soon find them again.' And she took the boy by the hand. He was not wearing mittens, but he was nice and warm.

'Now we must go and look at all the Christmas gnomes in the shop windows,' said the girl.

'Gnomes? What are they?' said the boy.

'Gnomes help Father Christmas to take round all the presents, of course!' laughed the girl. 'You'll soon see!' And off they went to the big store. There were Father Christmas masks hanging in all the windows and in the biggest window there was a train. A big toy train, with gnomes in all the carriages, and the train had real lights and travelled through tunnels and over bridges.

'There are the gnomes,' said the girl.

'Are all the carriages called gnomes?' asked the little boy.

'Oh no,' said the girl. 'It's the little men sitting in the carriages who are gnomes. Well, they're not really gnomes, because there are no such things as gnomes, it's just something we pretend about at Christmas time. Only very small children believe in gnomes.'

'Small children like me?' said the boy. 'Then I'm going to believe in gnomes.'

'Hello, Gnomes!' he called. What a shock! All the gnomes smiled and winked their eyes at the little boy. Everyone watching said: 'Oh, good heavens, fancy the gnomes being able to wink and smile! They really do think of extraordinary things to get people's money off them. Let's stay and see if they smile some more.' But the gnomes were sitting just as they had before, stiff-faced, in their little red caps, driving in and out of the tunnels. One of the smallest gnomes, sitting in the last carriage, was on the point of falling out. Every time the train had to swing round a bend to cross the bridge, he leaned further and further over to one side.

'Watch you don't fall, Gnome!' called the little boy, and the gnome gave a jerk and sat up straight and steady in the middle of the carriage. The people watching were quite beside themselves. 'Did you ever see such funny gnomes?' they shouted. 'They've made a really good job of the window display this year! Let's see if the other gnomes do something funny, too.' But the gnomes sat as stiff as sticks, driving along over the bridges and past the little stations.

'Look at the gnome stationmaster!' the boy cried suddenly, and a little stationmaster came out and blew his whistle and popped in again, almost before anyone had seen him.

'Oh, that was the best of all!' said the people watching. 'There must be somebody controlling it all from inside the shop. Wait a bit, and he'll come out again.' But the stationmaster did not come out again and the train continued to travel round bends and U-turns, through tunnels and over bridges.

'They must get tired of driving on and on and never stopping,' said the boy.

'Toys don't get tired,' said the girl, and the grown-ups laughed.

'Just fancy,' they said, 'that little boy thinks the gnomes are alive!'

'Now the gnomes are very tired,' the boy said. 'You can stop now!' he called to the gnomes, and the train stopped at once.

'It'll start off again soon,' said the people watching. 'We'd better stay here and wait for it.'

'It won't run again now. I asked the gnomes to stop it,' said the boy.

'Then you must ask them to go on again!' said the people, who were beginning to get quite cross.

'Well, drive on again, if you like,' said the boy, 'but I must go home now.' And the train began to move again.

The girl took the little boy by the hand and they walked down the road. 'Now you must tell me where you live,' she said.

'I live in Gnomeland!' laughed the boy. 'I'm a little gnome!'

'Oh no you're not!' said the girl. 'But how *did* you make the gnomes smile and do exactly what you told them?'

But the little boy just laughed.

'Goodbye!' he cried. 'Thank you, and a happy Christmas!' And he ran into a side road and disappeared.

Mrs Pepperpot gives a Christmas present

It was two days before Christmas. Mrs Pepperpot hummed and sang as she trotted round her kitchen, she was so pleased to be finished with all her Christmas preparations.

'How lovely that Christmas is here,' she said. 'Everybody's happy - especially the children – that's the best of all.'

The old woman was almost like a child herself because of this knack she had of suddenly shrinking to the size of a pepperpot.

She was thinking about all this while she was making her coffee, and she had just poured it into the cup when there was a knock at the door.

'Come in,' she said, and in came a little girl who was, oh, so pale and thin.

'Poor child! Wherever do you live – I'm sure I've never seen you before,' said Mrs Pepperpot.

'I'm Hannah. I live in the little cottage at the edge of the forest,' said the child, 'and I'm just going round to all the houses to ask if anybody has any old Christmas decorations left over from last year – glitter or paperchains or glass balls or anything, you know. Have *you* got anything you don't need?'

'I expect so, Hannah,' answered Mrs Pepperpot, and went up into the attic to fetch the cardboard box with all the decorations. She gave it to the little girl.

'How lovely! Can I really have all that?'

'You can,' said Mrs Pepperpot, 'and you shall have something else as well. Tomorrow I will bring you a big doll.'

'I don't believe that,' said Hannah.

'Why not?'

'You haven't *got* a doll.'

'That's simple; I'll buy one,' said Mrs

Pepperpot. 'I'll bring it over tomorrow afternoon, but I must be home by six o'clock at the latest, because it's Christmas Eve.'

'How wonderful if you can come tomorrow afternoon – I shall be all alone. Father and Mother both go out to work, you see, and they don't get back until the church bells have rung.'

So the little girl went home, and Mrs Pepperpot went down to the toy shop and bought a big doll. But when she woke up next morning there she was, once more, no bigger than a pepperpot.

'How provoking!' she said to herself. 'On this day of all days, when I have to take the doll to Hannah. Never mind! I expect I'll manage.'

After she had dressed she tried to pick up the doll, but it was much too heavy for her to lift.

I'll have to go without it, she thought, and opened the door to set off.

But, oh dear, it had been snowing hard all night, and the little old woman soon sank deep in the snowdrifts. The cat was sitting in front of the house; when she saw something moving in the snow she thought it was a mouse and jumped on it.

'Hi, stop!' shouted Mrs Pepperpot. 'Keep your claws to yourself! Can't you see it's just me shrunk again?'

'I beg your pardon,' said the cat, and started walking away.

'Wait a minute,' said Mrs Pepperpot, 'to make up for your mistake you can give me a ride down to the main road.' The cat was quite willing, so she lay down and let the little old woman climb on her back. When they got to the main road the cat stopped. 'Can you hear anything?' asked Mrs Pepperpot.

'Yes, I think it's the snowplough,' said the cat, 'so we'll have to get out of the way, or we'll be buried in snow.'

'I don't want to get out of the way,' said Mrs Pepperpot, and she sat down in the middle of the road and waited till the snowplough was right in front of her; then she jumped up and landed smack on the front tip of the plough.

There she sat, clinging on for dear life and

enjoying herself hugely. 'Look at me, the little old woman, driving the snowplough!' she laughed.

When the snowplough had almost reached the door of Hannah's little cottage, she climbed on to the edge nearest the side of the road and, before you could say 'Jack Robinson', she had landed safely on the great mound of snow thrown up by the plough. From there she could walk right across Hannah's hedge and slide down the other side. She was shaking the snow off her clothes on the doorstep when Hannah came out and picked her up.

'Are you the old woman who shrinks to the size of a pepperpot?'

'Of course I am, silly.'

'Where's the doll you were going to bring me?' asked Hannah when they got inside.

'I've got it at home. You'll have to go back with me and fetch it. It's too heavy for me.'

'Shouldn't you have something to eat, now that you've come to see me? Would you like a biscuit?' And the little girl held out a biscuit in the shape of a ring.

'Thank you very much,' said Mrs Pepperpot and popped her head through the biscuit ring.

Oh, how the little girl laughed! 'I quite forgot

you were so small,' she said.

They played games all afternoon, then Hannah put on her coat and with Mrs Pepperpot in her pocket she went off to fetch her doll.

'Oh, thank you!' she exclaimed when she saw it. 'But do you know,' she added, 'I would really rather have *you* to play with all the time.'

'You can come and see me again if you like,' said Mrs Pepperpot, 'I am often as small as a pepperpot, and then it's nice to have a little help around the house. And, of course, we can play games as well.'

So now the little girl often spends her time with Mrs Pepperpot. She looks ever so much better, and they often talk about the day Mrs Pepperpot arrived on the snowplough, and about the doll she gave Hannah.

Simon's Christmas present

It was the day before Christmas Eve and all over town the lights stayed on far into the night in houses great and small. And in the biggest house of all the windows were so bright that it looked like the king's own house. There was always someone running past the windows, some baking cakes, some making sausages and some pressing pickled pork.

And as they ran they shouted:

'Simon! Come and turn the doughnuts, Simon!'

'Simon! Cut some more sausage sticks, Simon!'

'Simon! Screw the pork press down a bit, Simon!'

And Simon turned the doughnuts and Simon cut the sausage sticks and Simon screwed down the pork press.

Christmas is the worst time of year, thought Simon. Everyone else loves Christmas, I'm the only one who thinks it's miserable.

And do you know why Simon felt like that? Well, it was because he had never been given a Christmas present. Of course, there are people who say that you shouldn't celebrate Christmas to get Christmas presents, but considering that a lot of grown-up people are very offended when they don't get presents, it was surely not surprising that Simon minded, since he was only a little boy and had neither a father nor a mother. Everyone could nag Simon as much as they liked.

But Simon had no time to stand about feeling sorry for himself for long.

There was a shout from the kitchen.

'Simon! Go down to the shed for wood, lots of wood. Hurry up now!'

Simon went, but he did not go very quickly and when he reached the woodshed and had to stretch up for the top logs, which were neatly stacked, he slipped and brought the whole woodpile down with him.

'Oh, bother it,' said Simon, and he sat down and rubbed his arm.

'Yes, me too!' came a voice from behind two logs which had fallen across each other.

Simon picked up one of the logs and there sat a little gnome, not much bigger than a kitten. It was dark in the woodshed, but round the gnome shone a red light, just as if the gnome himself was shining.

'No!' said Simon. 'Are you a real gnome?'

'Yes, as real as anything can be,' said the gnome, and taking out a little silver comb he began to tidy his hair, which had got in a mess when the woodpile tumbled down.

'I didn't mean to do it,' said Simon, looking sorry.

'It was just bad luck,' said the gnome. 'And now I must hurry home, because you know we've got to go out and deliver Christmas presents tomorrow night and they'll be waiting for me by now. I know you'll be happy tomorrow

night, when you get your Christmas present!'

'I haven't had a Christmas present since I can remember,' said Simon.

The gnome was so surprised that he almost dropped his silver comb. 'You don't get Christmas presents?' he said.

'No, I certainly do not,' said Simon.

'Then you shall have a Christmas present from me,' said the gnome, and he held out his comb to Simon.

'Oh no, that's really too much!' said Simon.

'Take it now, and I'll tell you something: when you're in the living room tomorrow evening and the Christmas presents are being handed out, comb your hair and you can have them all.'

'Oh, you are silly!' said Simon. 'You must have hit your head when you fell off the woodpile.'

'Oh no, I didn't,' said the gnome. 'This is a special comb, a lucky comb, but it hasn't been used yet. Here you are, happy Christmas and thanks, and now I must be off.'

In a flash the gnome had gone and Simon was left holding the comb in his hand.

There was a call from the kitchen door: 'Simon, bring the wood! Don't stand about dreaming the way you always do.'

And Simon did carry in the wood, humming and singing and filling up one wood box after another.

On Christmas Eve Simon sat with the other people of the house in the grand, freshly scoured living room – with the comb in his pocket. They would soon see some fun, when Simon began to comb his hair and wish for Christmas presents!

The farmer himself played Father Christmas. 'To the mother of the house,' said the farmer, bringing out the first present.

Shall I use the comb now? thought Simon. After all, she's often been so sour when I've overslept, she doesn't deserve a Christmas present.

But then he remembered the time when he had pneumonia and the farmer's wife had sat up with him night after night.

Oh well, she can have her present, I can wait, thought Simon.

'For the stable boy,' read the farmer.

Now we shall see some fun, thought Simon, because he couldn't bear the stable boy. It was he who had once pushed Simon into the stall with the big horse and laughed at him when he was frightened.

Simon took out the comb and was about to

49

use it, when he remembered that the stable boy had a lot of children waiting for him at home and the stable boy's parcel must be filled with pork ribs and sausages and honey cake. And Simon had just been eating pork rib and sausages and honey cake, so he could manage for now.

I shall use the lucky comb next time, thought Simon.

But he did nothing of the sort, for now farmer Christmas was reading out: 'To Simon the kitchen boy, pork-presser, wood-carrier, dough-

nut-turner and sausage-stick-cutter. Here you are, Simon! You've worked so hard all day today and yesterday that you deserve a Christmas present like the rest of us.'

Simon bowed and said thank you and when he opened the parcel there was a new box for his things from the farmer's wife, the stable boy had put in a gilded horseshoe and the farmer had bought him an elegant shirt wrapped up in cellophane. 'Well, for heaven's sake!' said Simon. 'And I didn't use the comb at all!'

'What comb are you talking about?' said farmer Christmas. 'You're washed so clean and your hair's so neat, you don't need a comb. And as I said, you've been so cheerful and good yesterday and today and if you are just as willing and easy to get on with next year there'll be a Christmas present then too!'

Then Simon remembered that it was after being given the comb that he had been so happy and hard working. He smiled until his face almost split in two.

It's a funny thing, but no one who gets a lucky comb will ever need to use it as long as he knows he has the comb in his pocket!

Mrs Pepperpot goes skiing

Mr Pepperpot had decided to go in for the annual local ski race. He had been a pretty good skier when he was young, so he said to Mrs Pepperpot: 'I don't see why I shouldn't have a go this year; I feel more fit than I have for many years.'

'That's right, Husband, you do that,' said Mrs Pepperpot, 'and if you win the cup you'll get your favourite ginger cake when you come home.'

So Mr Pepperpot put his name down, and when the day came he put on his white anorak and blue cap with a bobble on the top and strings under his chin. He slung his skis over his shoulders and said he would wax them when he got to the starting point.

'Righto! Best of luck!' said Mrs Pepperpot. She was already greasing the cake tin and stoking the stove for her baking.

'Thanks, Wife,' said Mr Pepperpot and went off. It was not until he had turned the corner by the main road that Mrs Pepperpot caught sight of his tin of wax which he had left on the top of the sideboard.

'What a dunderhead that man is!' exclaimed Mrs Pepperpot. She flung her shawl round her shoulders and trotted up the road as fast as she could with the tin of wax. When she got near the starting point there was a great crowd gathered. She dodged in and out to try and find her husband, but everyone seemed to be wearing white anoraks and blue caps. At last she saw a pair of sticks stuck in the snow with a blue cap hanging from the top. She could see the initials P.P. sewn in red thread inside.

That must be his cap, thought Mrs Pepperpot. Those are his initials, Peter Pepperpot. I sewed them on myself in red thread like that. I'll just drop the wax in the cap; then he'll find it when he comes to pick up his sticks.

As she bent forward to put the wax in the cap she accidentally knocked it off the stick and at that moment she shrank so quickly that it was she who fell into the cap, while the tin of wax rolled out into the snow!

And a moment later a big hand reached down, snatched up the cap and crammed it over a mop of thick hair. Mrs Pepperpot was trapped!

'Number 46!' she heard the starter shout, 'on your mark, get set, go!' And Number 46, with

Mrs Pepperpot in his cap, glided off to a smooth start.

Somebody must have lent him some wax, she thought; there's nothing wrong with his skis, anyway. Then from under the cap she shouted, 'Don't overdo it, now, or you'll have no breath left for the spurt at the end!'

She could feel the skier slow up a little. 'I suppose you know who's under your cap?' she added. 'You had forgotten the wax, so I brought it along. Only I fell into your cap instead of the wax.'

Mrs Pepperpot now felt the skier's head turn round to see if anyone was talking to him from behind.

'It's me, you fool!' said Mrs Pepperpot. 'I've shrunk again. You'll have to put me off by the lane to our house – you pass right by, re-member?'

But the skier had stopped completely now.

'Come on, man, get a move on!' shouted Mrs Pepperpot. 'They'll all be passing you!'

'Is it . . . is it true that you're the little old woman who shrinks to the size of a pepper-pot?'

'Of course – you know that!' laughed Mrs Pepperpot.

'Am *I* married to *you*? Is it *my* wife who shrinks?'

'Yes, yes, but hurry now!'

'No,' said the skier, 'if that's how it is I'm not going on with the race at all.'

'Rubbish!' shouted Mrs Pepperpot. 'You *must* go on! I put a cake in the oven before I went out and if it's scorched it'll be all your fault!'

But the skier didn't budge.

'Maybe you'd like me to pop out of your cap and show myself to everybody? Any minute now I might go back to my full size and then the cap will burst and the whole crowd will see who is married to the shrinking woman. Come on, now! With any luck you may just do it, but there's no time to lose. Hurry!'

This worked; the skier shot off at full speed, helping himself to take huge strides with his sticks. 'Fore!' he shouted as he sped past the other skiers. But when they came to the refreshment stall Mrs Pepperpot could smell the lovely hot soup, and she thought her husband deserved a break. 'We're well up now,' she called. 'You could take a rest.'

The skier slowed down to a stop and Mrs Pepperpot could hear there were many people standing round him. 'Well done!' they said.

'You're very well placed. But what are you looking so worried about? Surely you're not frightened of the last lap, are you?'

'No, no, nothing like that!' said the skier. 'It's this cap of mine – I'm dead scared of my cap!'

Under the cap Mrs Pepperpot was getting restless again. 'That's enough of that!' she called. 'We'll have to get on now!'

The people who stood nearest heard the voice and wondered who spoke. The woman who ladled out the soup said, 'Probably some loud-speaker.'

And Mrs Pepperpot couldn't help laughing. 'Nearer the truth than you think!' she thought. Then she called out again, 'Come on, Husband,

put that spurt on, and let's see if we can make it!'

And the skis shot away again, leaping many yards each time the sticks struck into the snow. Very soon Mrs Pepperpot could hear the sound of clapping and cheering.

'What do we do now?' whispered the skier in a miserable voice. 'Can you last another minute? Then I can throw the cap off under the fir trees just before we reach the finishing line.'

'Yes, that will be all right,' said Mrs Pepperpot. And, as the skis sped down the last slope, the strings were untied and the cap flew through the air, landing safely under the fir trees.

When Mrs Pepperpot had rolled over and

over many times she found herself growing big once more. So she got up, shook the snow off her skirt and walked quietly home to her house.

The cake was only a little bit burnt on the top when she took it out of the oven, so she cut off the black part and gave it to the cat. Then she whipped some cream to put on top and made a steaming pot of coffee to have ready for her champion husband.

Sure enough, Mr Pepperpot soon came home *without* the cup. 'I forgot to take the wax,' he said, 'so I didn't think it was worth going in for the race. But I watched it, and you should have seen Paul Petersen today; I've never seen him run like that in all my born days. All the same, he looked very queer, as if he'd seen a ghost or something.'

Then Mrs Pepperpot began to laugh. And ever since, when she's feeling sad or things are not going just right, all she has to do is to remember the day she went ski racing in the wrong cap, and then she laughs and laughs and laughs.

Christmas Eve with the Mouse family

Every Christmas Eve, Mother Mouse and the children swept and dusted their whole house, and for a Christmas tree Father Mouse decorated an old boot with a spider's web and little nails. They ate sweet papers and a little nut each and sniffed at a piece of bacon fat.

After that, they danced round and round the boot, and sang and played games till they were tired out. Then Father Mouse would say: 'That's all for tonight! Time to go to bed!'

That is how it had been every Christmas and that is how it was to be this year. The little mice held each other by the tail and danced round the boot, while Granny Mouse sat rocking to and fro on a potato, enjoying the fun.

But when Father Mouse said, 'Time for bed!' all the children dropped each other's tails and shouted: 'No! No!'

'What's that?' said Father Mouse. 'When I say it's time for bed, you children have to go to bed, while I stand guard!'

'No, no!' wailed the children, and climbed on to Granny's knee. She hugged them all lovingly. 'Why don't you want to go to bed, my sugar lumps?'

'Because we want to go upstairs to the big drawing room and dance round a proper Christmas tree,' said the eldest Mouse child. 'You see, I've been peeping through a crack in the wall and I saw a huge Christmas tree with lots and lots of lights on it.'

'Oh, but the drawing room can be a very dangerous place for mice,' said Granny.

'Not when all the people have gone to bed,' objected the eldest Mouse child.

'Oh, do let's go!' they all pleaded.

'Perhaps we could take them up there just for a minute or two,' suggested Mother Mouse.

'Very well,' said Father, 'but follow me closely.'

So they set off. They tiptoed past three tins of herring, two large jars of jam and a barrel of cider.

'We have to go very carefully here,' whispered Father Mouse, 'not to knock over any bottles. Are you all right, Granny?'

'Of course I'm all right,' said Granny.

'Mind the trap!' said the eldest Mouse child. 'It's behind that sack of potatoes.'

'I know that,' said Granny; 'it's been there

Oh, how lovely!

since I was a child. I'm not afraid of that!' And she took a flying leap right over the trap and scuttled after the others up the wall.

'What a lovely tree!' cried all the children when they peeped out of the hole by the drawing room fireplace. 'But where are the lights? You said there'd be lights, didn't you?'

'There were lights last night,' said the eldest. 'But now it's dark.'

They stood looking for a little while. Then suddenly a whole lot of coloured lights lit up the tree! By accident, Granny had touched the electric switch by the fireplace.

'Oh, how lovely!' they all exclaimed, and

Father and Mother and Granny thought it was very nice too. They walked right round the tree, looking at the decorations, the little paper baskets and the glass balls. But the children found something even more exciting: a mechanical lorry!

Of course, they couldn't wind it up themselves, but its young master had wound it up before he went to bed, to be ready for him to play with in the morning. So when the Mouse children clambered into it, it started off right away.

'Children, children! You mustn't make such a noise!' warned Mother Mouse.

But the children didn't listen; they were having a wonderful time going round and round and round in the lorry.

'As long as the cat doesn't come!' said Father Mouse anxiously.

He had hardly spoken before the cat walked silently through the open door.

Father, Mother and Granny Mouse all made a dash for the hole in the skirting but the children were trapped in the lorry. They had never been so scared in all their mouse lives.

Then the lorry started slowing down. 'I think we'd better make a jump for it and try to get up

in the tree,' said the eldest Mouse child.

One hid in a paper basket, another behind a bulb (which nearly burned him), a third swung on a glass ball and the fourth rolled himself up in some cotton wool. But where was the eldest Mouse? Oh yes, he had climbed right to the top and was balancing next to the star and shouting at the cat:

'Silly, silly cat,
You can't catch us!
You're much too fat,
Silly, silly cat!'

But the cat pretended not to hear or see the little mice. She sharpened her claws on the lorry. 'I'm not interested in catching mice tonight,' she said as if to herself, 'I only want to play with the lorry.'

'Pooh! That's just a story!' said the eldest. 'You'd catch us quick enough if we came down.'

'Not on Christmas Eve!' said the cat. So the little mice jumped down again and the cat did not touch them. All she said was: 'Hurry back to your hole now, I'll be after you again once Christmas Eve is over.'

The little mice pelted back to their hole, where Father and Mother and Granny Mouse were waiting for them and made them promise never to go up to the drawing room again.